NoGBAD
and the Elephants

For Prue

EGMONT
We bring stories to life

First published in Great Britain 1967.
This edition first published in Great Britain 2016 by Egmont UK Limited
The Yellow Building, 1 Nicholas Road, London W11 4AN
www.egmont.co.uk

Text copyright © The Estate of Oliver Postgate 1967
Illustrations copyright © Peter Firmin 1967
The moral rights of the illustrator have been asserted.

ISBN 978 1 4052 8142 3

A CIP catalogue record for this title is available from the British Library.

Stay safe online.
Egmont is not responsible for content hosted by third parties.

FSC

MIX
Paper
FSC® C018306

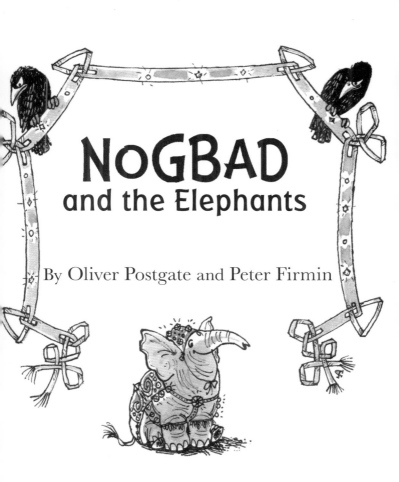

NoGBAD
and the Elephants

By Oliver Postgate and Peter Firmin

EGMONT

This is the castle of Noggin the Nog.
Noggin the Nog lived here a long time ago.

This is another castle.
Nogbad the Bad lived here.

Nogbad the Bad stayed in his castle,
but his crows flew about.
His crows flew everywhere.
His crows saw everything.

Nogbad's crows saw this strange monster
with jewels on its coat.
It was walking over the hills
to Noggin's castle.

"What is this monster?" cried the Nogs.
The monster's keeper said, "It is a birthday
present for Noggin's son, a birthday present
for Prince Knut from the King of Southland.
Please lead me to Prince Knut."

The keeper bowed to Prince Knut.
He said, "My master, the King of Southland,
wishes you a happy birthday
and sends you this small present."

Noggin said, "We thank you for this
rich present.
The monster is rare and strange.
It has a coat with many jewels, but its
face is sad.
Why is its face so sad?"

The keeper said, "I do not know.
Perhaps the monster is cold.
Perhaps it is tired.
It is only a baby monster.
Perhaps it did not want to go away
from its mother."

Nogbad's crow heard all they said.
Then it flew away through the forest.

It flew to Nogbad's black castle
on the hilltop.

The crow told Nogbad about the monster
with the sad face and about its coat
with many jewels.
"What can this monster be?" said Nogbad.
They looked in a big book about animals.
"That monster is an elephant," said Nogbad,
"a baby elephant. I am going to steal that
elephant's coat with many jewels."

17

Soon it was time for the elephant's keeper to
go home.
Knut and the elephant waved goodbye
as he rode away on a donkey.

Knut and the elephant played games.
They played hide and seek.
They played hunt the helmet.
They played sardines and ran races with the
soldiers, but still the elephant was sad.

Knut said to Noggin,
"The baby elephant is still sad.
What can we do to make it happy?"
Noggin said, "Perhaps it will cheer up
if we make a big bonfire."

Nooka brought blankets to cover it with.
Noggin brought hot water bottles to warm
it with.

The baby elephant did not cheer up.
It lay down by the fire and went to sleep.
"I will sit with it until it wakes up,"
said Knut.

"Listen," said Noggin, "I can hear
a noise like a trumpet."

The baby elephant heard it too.
It woke up and lifted its ears.

The soldiers ran in.

"A monster is coming!" they shouted.

"A monster like that one, but much bigger.

It is coming this way!"

The noise grew louder.

The ground shook as the trumpeting
monster came near.
The Nogs were afraid and hid, but the baby
elephant smiled and flapped its ears.

In through the castle gate came
a huge grey elephant.
It clanked.
It banged and rattled.
It trumpeted.

The baby elephant smiled.

The baby elephant laughed.

The baby elephant danced
around the big elephant.

Together the two elephants went out
through the castle gates.

Noggin and Nooka watched the elephants
go away.
"Perhaps that is its mother who has come to
take it home. It looks very happy now."

Together the two elephants walked
through the forest.
They walked along the path by
the river that leads to Nogbad's castle.

34

The happy baby elephant
wanted to swim.
It ran down into the river.

It blew water on its back.

It blew bubbles.
Elephants love to swim
in the river.

The baby elephant wanted the big elephant
to come and swim in the river.
The big elephant did not seem to want
to bathe.
The baby elephant took hold of the big
elephant's trunk.
It pulled the big elephant's trunk.

The big elephant split in half.
There, inside the frame of wood
and torn cloth, sat Nogbad the Bad.

The baby elephant was angry –
very, very angry.
It filled its trunk with water
and blew it at Nogbad.

41

Nogbad ran away.

The elephant chased him.

Nogbad ran fast, but the elephant ran faster.

It caught Nogbad and carried him to Noggin.
"Put him in prison," said Noggin.

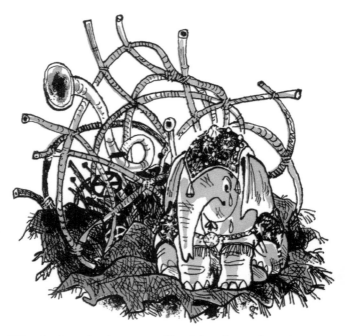

The baby elephant walked back to the river.
It sat by the bits of Nogbad's elephant.
The baby elephant was very sad.
It wept.

Knut said, "The baby elephant is sad
because it wants to be with its mother.
I will take it back to its mother
in the Southland."

Nooka made the elephant
some thick woolly socks.

She made it a big coat
of sheep's wool.

"Goodbye, baby elephant," shouted the Nogs.
"Look after him, Knut! Goodbye."

Knut and the elephant set off for
the Southland.

The end